WED TO THE BULLMAN

ARRANGED MONSTER MATES

BOOK NINE

EDEN EMBER

❀ Created with Vellum

PREQUEL

No one remembers the world before the Shift. It was thousands of years ago, all lost, all forgotten. Scientists and historians say that before, the world was better, brighter, and our planet belonged to us, humans. There were proud countries and bustling cities, and technology was at its highest.

We can hardly imagine all that. There is no proof, no written texts, no pictures of Alia Terra before the Shift. All we know is the face of Alia Terra now. The land haphazardly divided into territories, the walled cities, the poor living on the fringes, barely surviving.

The monsters.

The temples where young virgins can take a DNA test and be matched to one of them. An arranged marriage to a monster is often the only way a woman can save herself or give her family a chance to not starve.

This is Alia Terra. It belongs to the monsters, and we belong to them.

CHAPTER 1

*V*ozak

"This is very unconventional. We normally put the DNA into the database, and the computer finds the match." The nurse shakes her head while drawing my blood and swabbing my mouth. Auryn stands beside me, dictating where she should look.

"I know, but I'm a match to his brother. My little Sister Agnes is waiting for her match. I figured they'd be a match. And yeah, I'm biased. I want her here with me." Auryn is convincing.

"Okay, I'll send it through for your sister first."

I blow out a deep breath—this is a new thing for me. Coming to Earth wasn't in the plans as I was to stay with our parents. But seeing how happy and fulfilled Vrakius was, along with his sweet wife and child, I wanted to experience it too. And actually, my mother and father encouraged me to leave Tariat. So I did. I waited for a while to submit the DNA test. Honestly, I wasn't really sure I wanted a wife. But Vrakius talked me into it.

Two weeks go by and they tell me I have a match. It's not the same nurse who informs me, and they don't tell me her name, only that I need to get to the marriage temple to pick her up if I accept. According to the document, she's a perfect match.

Auryn wrings her hands as I prepare for the trip. Her family doesn't have comms and can't communicate with the outside world. They rely on written mail and courier services, or she'd ask them.

"Listen, even if it's not Agnes, you need to treat her well." Vrakius means well, but he's an overbearing brother.

I square my shoulders. "I know, brother. I'm not, as the humans say, an idiot."

My brother pats my shoulder. "Yes, I know you're not. But go easy. You are gruff at times."

"It's the minotaur way." I'm quite proud of my heritage. Minotaurs aren't fluffy little pets. We're big and brutish and bold. My wife must adjust to the creature I am. Vrakius grew too soft in my opinion.

"I'll be cordial."

Auryn gives me a worried look. "If your mate is Agnes, you better treat her well."

"He better treat her well regardless of who she is," Vrakius corrects.

I hop into the old truck Vrakius let me borrow. He says it's a good luck truck since he picked up Auryn in it. The road to the temple stretches before me—it will take a good day to get there. We don't have access to hovercrafts like others do. The minotaurs are ranchers here, living simple and primitive lives.

The road to the temple becomes engorged with traffic. Vessels land at the nearby airfield, and many different male beings arrive. I'm not alone in this. The marriage temple is the perfect way to match the aliens to the humans. Apparently, they refer to me as an alien. I snort—I'm a minotaur, not an alien.

"You're early, Vozak. Your human doesn't arrive until tomorrow." The older human female glances at her clipboard and offers a smile.

"I was told to come right away to the temple to pick up my wife." This is turning out to be a big waste of time. I have ground to till and livestock to feed. I left Vrakius with the task of feeding my livestock, but he doesn't have time to touch my fallow ground.

"I'm sorry about that. We process many marriages a day. You're a minotaur, so we have the magistrate for your ceremony. You'll have to come back tomorrow for processing. She's just getting on the train now."

I nod and turn, but then I turn back. "What is her name?"

She glances at her clipboard. "Agnes. Agness Ridgewood. She's coming from the eastern seaboard settlement."

My heart pounds at the mention of Auryn's sister's name. I smile, nod, and leave, heading into the walled city to find a room for the night.

"Vozak? Well?" Auryn's voice cracks through my comm.

I chuckle. "You better prepare a big welcome party for your sister."

She squeals so loudly, I pull the comm away.

"I can't believe this! Yes! Are you sure it's our Agnes?"

"Agnes Ridgewood. Can't be any other, can there?"

"No! Oh, you have made my day, my year! Honey, Agnes is his wife." She hollers at Vrakius.

"Not yet. She's coming in tomorrow. I'm in the city for the night." I huff sounding impatient.

"Aw, well, you'll be fresh for her tomorrow. I guarantee you she's on cloud nine."

"She is?" My brow furrows as I have no idea where cloud nine is.

Auryn laughs. "It means she's super happy. She wanted to meet you and hoped you'd be her match. She was rather taken by Vrakius."

"Hmph." I hope she isn't still taken by him. I will not compete with my brother for my mate's attention. "She better be taken with me when we marry." My gruffness comes through the comm.

"Oh, Vozak, I forget how literal you are. I mean she really thinks highly of Vrakius and minotaurs. She wants a minotaur for her husband. When she found out we were bringing you back, she got all excited. And look, it worked like a charm."

"That it did. Auryn, you knew. I'll be home tomorrow evening with my new wife and your sister."

Auryn sighs. "Listen, Vozak, at least stop along the way. Give her a good honeymoon. I know you minotaurs like to get back to your ranches and work, but the human female loves some attention. Be kind and gentle with her. She's my baby sister. I want her to arrive fresh-faced and happy to be your bride, okay?"

It's not much to ask, I know. But my brother's wife is very controlling about her sister, and she seems to think I don't know how to treat a human female. I've read the human history and physiology books. The marriage temple sends them out when an alien has testing for a DNA match. I think I know how to operate Agnes.

CHAPTER 2

*a*gnes

Every day I wait for the courier to bring news, and every day I'm superbly disappointed. I'm beginning to think I'll be the old maid of the family since the marriage temple hasn't found a DNA match. Auryn and Chelsea have their mates and children, of all things. I trudge to the front of our apartment building and step onto the sidewalk, watching people walk by heading to their jobs and the markets.

The little van pulls up with the words Courier Service painted on the side. My heart skips a beat as he walks to our building.

"Who are you looking for?" I ask, surprising him because he didn't notice me walking by.

"Agnes Ridgewood."

"I'm here." I nearly jump up and down as he hands me the large packet from the Marriage Temple. The words are big and bold. You Have A Match!

"Mother! Guess what?" I tear into our tiny apartment yelling. She's in the kitchen canning vegetables. I really should be helping her, but there's really not much room for two doing it. She shooed me away earlier.

"You have a match?" Her eyes are bright and wide, but her voice is forced, almost flat. She'd been through this twice already with my two older sisters. Now it's my turn.

I run to Mother's arms while she holds back her tears. "You don't have to be brave, mom. It's okay."

She rears back and smiles despite it. "I'm both sad and happy, for three reasons. One, sad to see you go. Two, happy to see you get your dream. Three, happy dad and I can rightfully retire now that our children have left the nest."

This was news. I perch on the old worn-out sofa. "Oh? What will you do? Where will you go?"

"We want a hovel outside of the city. Someplace where we can grow our food and have peace and quiet. We applied when Auryn sent her DNA to the marriage temple. We received a letter stating we'd have our request as soon as our children grew up and moved on."

"Who is your match? Is it Vozak?"

I read the letter. "All it says is they found a DNA match, and I'm to come to the marriage temple. It doesn't say who or what they are." I frown because this is important information. It doesn't really matter at this point since my DNA match is already on his way to the temple to marry me.

Somehow, their intentions make it easier for me to leave. Honestly, all I do here is mope around the tiny apartment or go out into our community and see all the other unhappy people waiting for their dreams to come true.

Daddy beams all the way to the train station. I turn to him and grab his arm. "Aren't you going to miss me?"

"Oh, little princess, of course, we will. But you need to understand, we're using the freedom to move to make it easier on us. We're not losing a daughter; we're gaining freedom. We've always wanted to live in the country, have our own land, but we couldn't as long as we were raising children. We had to live close to the schools. Now we can retire, and our children are starting their own families."

"How will we know where you are? The couriers don't go to the countryside."

"We'll send word, much the same way we communicate with Auryn and Chelsea."

"I think we should get you a comm."

"Oh, those are so expensive." Mom always has a reason why she can't do something.

"All the aliens use them."

"They're loaded, we aren't. We'll send our address with the central courier. The people living in the rural areas have access; we just have to go to the office in order to send and receive mail."

The train wailed its call. I nearly missed it. By the time they load my suitcases, I have one minute to say my goodbyes.

"Oh, baby girl, go forth and have a wonderful life. Get married, have babies, and be happy."

My face turns to the train window, watching the landscape go by. Sleepy communities, walled cities, alien territories giving me a fresh perspective on the world. I've not seen much beyond the walled human colony on the eastern seaboard. I have seen the ocean and the beach, but there's a colony of amphibian aliens that has claimed most of that area.

I mostly slept overnight and woke up as the train pulled into the walled city near the marriage temple. Others sleepily rise from their seats. I need to change so I will look presentable to my new husband. My wrist is vacant of a comm while so many travelers have them. My sisters and I come from the poorest part of Alia Terra.

An old bus and an alien driver wait to pick up the females from the train and carry us to the temple. They usher us into a large room which thankfully has restrooms.

"May I dress?"

"Time for that in a minute," the older lady says and motions for me to sit with the others.

After explaining what will happen when we go through the ceremony, she hands us our cards with the name of the male and the type of alien he is. The sealed envelope contains my future.

"You may use the facility to prepare. The ceremonies will start momentarily. We go in alphabetical order."

No problem, I have plenty of time to prepare as I walk to the facility with my bags and the envelope. I duck inside a stall and nervously open the envelope as I'm sitting on the toilet. A giggle passes from my lips at the audacity of reading who my husband will be while I'm peeing.

Alien Species: Minotaur

Name: Vozak Tarvir

I squeal out of excitement and giggle again.

"Are you okay?" The lady next to me asks.

"Yes. I'm quite well. I just found out I'm marrying a minotaur that happens to be the brother of my sister's minotaur husband."

"Wow, what good luck!"

The simple sleeveless dress hugs my youthful curves. Both Auryn and Chelsea helped me make the dress while we worked together on our wedding dresses. It hung in the back of my closet for months, and I considered selling it, thinking I'd missed my chance and wouldn't find a match.

I perch on the edge of the old hardwood pew that probably served in an old church somewhere prior. Or maybe this grand temple was once one of the churches from before the fall. Judging by the stained glass windows that line the place, I'd guess that's exactly what it was. They call my name, and my heart pounds as I follow the woman through the giant sanctuary doors.

CHAPTER 3

*V*ozak

Patience isn't my strongest character. I pace back and forth in front of the crowd of aliens in the room. They call us out when it's our turn, and our special officiant performs the ceremonies.

"Vozak Tarvir."

Finally. Dust particles stream through the sunlight from the giant stain-glass windows. I stand next to the magistrate, a tall being with a thick bulbous head on top. His long white mustache droops down and twitches as he smiles.

This female is supposed to be my perfect DNA match. Auryn and Vrakius get along beautifully. I stand tall when the door opens at the opposite end of the sanctuary.

The young lady steps through, her wide eyes searching and lands on me. A small smile stretches across her beautiful face. She indeed looks similar to Auryn. My chin lifts as we

13

lock eyes. The moment turns uncomfortable as I'm not accustomed to being under such scrutiny. The absence of the chase and capture of a female minotaur makes me mourn for the primal urges that won't happen. It can't happen with a human female. I read the booklet about how human females are. Plus, Vrakius gave me a good talk before I left.

The moment she steps close, her scent reaches my nose. A mixture of flowers and her essence, something sweet, something that riles my body, causes my cock to stand at attention. Quickly, I shift so I don't look like I'm ready to throw her down and do her right here. Inwardly, I chuckle over the aliens that require public intercourse and mating to prove they're married. I'm game for it, no shame in doing what comes naturally.

The magistrate looks at us and nods to the woman who led Agnes to me. "Agnes Ridgewood, this is Vozak Tarvir, a minotaur of the Taurus Territory."

She nods at me with a sweet smile, and I gaze upon her slight frame, her petite body and curves with great approval. Claiming her later will be easy enough.

"Gather your hands," the magistrate commands.

She offers a smile with her hands and holds them to me. My own are rough, calloused from doing ranch work, large because I'm a minotaur. Her hands are small, soft, and trembling. She's trembling! I'll break her for sure when we mate. Perhaps we need to figure out a way that I won't hurt her.

"Promises made are as good as gold and strong as stone. Never break them." The magistrate looks at us as he speaks. "Do you promise to adhere to one another, through all life, through all sickness, through all health, never parting, never giving sway to a wandering eye?"

"I promise," Agnes says and looks at me.

"Yes, I promise," I say, my voice gruffer than I intend.

"And do you both promise to create a family, to replenish Alia Terra with a new breed, to live and love and always work together until death takes one?"

Agnes' face turns sour, but she nods. "Yes, I promise."

"I promise." I stand tall, taking it like a true minotaur.

"By the authority placed on me through the governing land of Alia Terra, I call you husband and wife. You are now officially married. Step to the back for the signature and filing of your status."

And just like that, that quickly, it is over. I drop her hands and grab the official document, taking it to the room in the back of the sanctuary. Agnes follows on my heels. She says nothing as they sign it, stamp it, and officially file it in the central computer. We carry a copy with us and leave as a married couple.

I lead her to the old truck, and she looks at me. "You are Vrakius' brother? You know my sister, Auryn?"

"I do." The key starts the truck, and we take off heading south.

She sits quietly beside me, her eyes taking in the land as we drive.

"You are quiet."

"Yes. I tend to get this way when I'm with someone who doesn't like to talk." She doesn't look at me.

I sigh. I've done it again, and I'm sure I'll hear about it once Agnes talks to her sister about me. "Are you hungry?"

Her lower lip pulls between her teeth. "I'm really nervous. Not so hungry. But obviously, you need food. So do what you need to do."

I nod. "Okay, we'll drive for a while."

"Vozak, are you happy you did this?"

I look at her as my brow furrows. "This is what's expected of me. When I came to Alia Terra, I agreed to seek a wife. I am here to help my people multiply and have a good presence."

She nods. "I see. So this isn't something you dreamed about happening all your life? It's just a duty to your people, right?" Her eyes bore into me.

I answer without turning my head. "Yes."

She stiffens, looking in the opposite direction of me. I sense something isn't right with her.

CHAPTER 4

Agnes

Fighting back tears, I glare out the passenger window to avoid him. Now, I wish I hadn't begged Auryn to have her brother-in-law tested. Now, Auryn brings a smile to my face. If anything, being close to her will be my reason for living. Not that I'm suicidal. I read too many books about the olden days, when people met and fell in love with their soulmates and lived happily ever after. At this rate, I don't think I'll get my happily-ever-after with Vozak. He's too matter-of-fact. It must be a cultural difference. I need to discuss this with Auryn.

He grunts. "Mmph. Hungry." It's not a question really, more of a statement. The minotaur is hungry, therefore, we will stop and eat.

I say nothing as he pulls into a lot to a giant restaurant. It's a cafeteria-style offering cuisine for All. The sign boasts different aliens, and a human is in the mix. Good. That means there will be some weirdness involved. Hopefully, they cater to humans too.

Vozak comes around to my side. Well, that's gentlemanly of him. He isn't one for words. With a grunt, he turns to the cafeteria, and I follow behind like a good little wife. We haven't consummated the marriage yet. That will come, and I'm nervous about how that will work. Can I live the rest of my life with a business-only husband? I suppose I'll have to, no choice. Although, the marriage temple human representative said we can get out of it if we so choose. The magistrate made us promise to stick together no matter what. I wish he had put something in there about being kind and gentle and loving.

Vozak grabs a tray and goes right to work filling it with the foods he sees. The minotaur has a healthy appetite. I'm not used to being disregarded like this. My father always put my mom and his daughters first when we did anything. This monster just plows ahead like the world owes him a big meal.

I choose from the vegetables and the meats I recognize. I even like the boarius since Auryn and Vrakius brought us some when they visited. Vozak glances behind him and sees the slice on my tray and snorts.

"You like boarius?"

"I do," I say dryly.

He sits at a table and starts shoveling the food into his mouth. "Mmm." He truly enjoys his food.

I pick at my food. My nerves have the best of me. I wish the honeymoon, such as it is, were over, and I knew what to expect. I can't imagine it will be anything tender, like lying in each other's arms, kissing, and saying sweet nothings. Too many romance novels from the days of old have ruined my perception.

"You like your food?" He nods at my tray.

"It's okay." I force myself to eat it, though my belly churns with anticipation.

"You're a minotaur of few words. The silence is deafening." I look at my new husband, searching for some semblance of affection or happiness.

He grunts. A small amused smile stretches across his face. "It's loud in here. Are you going deaf?"

I laugh. Our differences in language are great. "It's a figure of speech."

"Oh yeah. I forget humans often say things that aren't real. It's weird. What do you mean? Silence is deafening."

My head tilts as I study his face and try to read his expression. "I mean, you aren't talkative, at all. We just met and we should talk to get to know each other. It's quite different from when Vrakius and Auryn married."

Laughter disguised as a grunt comes from him. "I'm not Vrakius. He came here ready to find a wife, ready to marry. I'm not acclimated to this planet yet. Minotaurs do things differently on Tariat."

"This isn't Tariat, and I'm not a minotaur." My eyes bore into his. I'll fight for my happiness if that's what it takes.

"Clearly. And we have a lot to learn from one another."

"Yes. Yay, you agree on that. It starts with conversations. Being so silent all the time isn't getting the job done." My brow lifts.

"I don't talk much. I work, I do what I'm supposed to do. I eat, sleep, and work."

I giggle nervously. "That's good and all, but now you have a mate, a wife. There's no need for just working and eating."

"What are we supposed to do then?"

"Well, we get to know each other. Enjoy ourselves. Discover what makes us tick. Have fun in the process. Maybe take up hobbies, visit family and friends. I don't know, Vozak. We just met, just married. I know nothing about you except that you don't like to talk, and you feel everything you do is your duty. Like, do you even enjoy life?"

He shrugs. "I'm trying. Is that good enough? I'm trying to learn the ways here. It's a new place, a new way of doing things. I tested for a DNA match because I thought I was ready for a wife. And Auryn was also pressuring me. I'm trying, Agnes. Maybe you and I will get along as the days go by. I'm sorry if I'm not what you expected."

Oh boy. "Let me ask you this, am I what you expected?"

"You are more than I expected. I'm trying to figure out how to do this. It's new to me, just like it is for you."

Maybe I'm being too hard on him. I reach across the table and touch his hand and smile. "Then we'll figure this out together."

He smiles and nods. "Yes. Are you ready to move on? We have a long trip."

Outside the golden sun sinks low in the west, casting long shadows. It's been a long day. I'm growing weary after sleeping on the train the night before.

"Will we stop for the night or drive straight through?"

CHAPTER 5

Vozak

"We can stop if you need the rest. Otherwise, I'm good to drive through."

"No, please stop. I slept last night on the train, sitting up. I'm very tired right now."

We pull into a walled city along the deep river that was once called Mississippi. Now, the minotaurs refer to it as the River Longus. Others call it something different. I can't remember what. The walled city perches next to it, with a wide tall bridge leading to the other territories.

I drive until I find an Inn near the River Longus. It's perched upon a steep bank with patios that look out over the natural beauty of the place. At least, it puts a smile on my wife's lips.

Agnes looks around with an occasional giggle escaping her lips. She says it's nerves. Maybe so. Once we're in our room overlooking the River Longus, she sets her bags on the chest of drawers and perches on the bed, looking around as if someone were about to jump out at her.

"I need a shower." She jumps up quickly and disappears in the bathroom. I relax on the bed, scrolling through my tablet I brought from Tariat. I'm so engrossed in the reading I don't catch when Agnes emerges.

She floats to me wearing a white gown, very see-through. Her curves poke out, giving me a glimpse of her naked body. She looks at me and bites her lower lip.

"Do you need a shower?"

I shrug. Then Auryn's voice comes into my head.

"Remember to bathe. Humans like a nice clean body to kiss."

Instantly my cock engorges at the thought of Agnes' lips on my body. I blush and rise heading to the bathroom for a quick shower. When I emerge, Agnes lies in the bed, the covers pulled back and she smiles at me, patting the bed beside her. Then she sees I'm completely naked and her eyes widen exponentially, her mouth falling agape as her eyes wander over my ripped body. That's what Auryn says about minotaurs, that we have ripped bodies and that her little sister likes that about us.

She swallows hard and sits up, her eyes on my cock which grows, standing erect from the attention. "Wow."

"How do humans do this?" Auryn didn't go into detail and all Vrakius said was that it would come naturally.

Her nervous giggle bubbles forth. "I don't know. I'm a virgin. All I have to compare to are the romance novels I read. But those were about humans. How do minotaurs do it?"

"Like this, come here." My body dictates the desire flowing heavily through my veins right now. I want to mate, I want to make her my wife and fill her with my seed.

She comes to me, timid, unsure. I reach out and flip her around and bend her over the bed while lifting the gown. "What? No!" She whips around on me, her eyes wide and wild. "Maybe minotaurs mount their mates, but I'm not a cow."

I throw my hands up. "How do humans do it?"

She lies back on the bed, a seductive smile on her beautiful face. "More like this. You get on top of me. And well, make love to me."

I laugh. "If I did that, I'd squish you flat. Here, scoot to the edge of the bed."

She looks down, a pained expression crossing her face. But she scoots to the edge and glares up at me.

"What? What's wrong?"

"We're newlyweds. Could you at least show me some affection? We haven't even kissed yet, ever. And you just want to jump in and have intercourse without any of the fun."

I sigh heavily. My cock is about to explode. I grasp it, give it a quick squeeze and release it, trying to clear my thoughts.

"Minotaurs aren't really the affectionate type. We're virile, we like to mount our mates and make babies. This affection thing is new to us. I've seen Auryn and Vrakius and the others on the ranches do it. Maybe you could teach me?" I offer a smile.

"Okay. Sit down beside me." She slips her gown off revealing her naked body, pale skin soft and clean. Turning to me, she smiles.

"Look at me. Touch me. I won't break." Her hand reaches for me, rubbing over my shoulder and chest.

I moan, the action stirring odd emotions. She smiles and moves closer, until her face is right in front of mine.

"Kiss me, silly minotaur."

I grab her shoulders and bring her to me, leaning in I close the gap, my lips landing on hers. Sweet, soft, supple, and the taste of berries on her soft tongue that gingerly protrudes touching mine. I like it, the emotions stir in my heart and low in my belly, my cock responding by growing harder. She moves until she's sitting on my lap. Her soft skin against my own lowers any walls I may have built around my heart. Suddenly, I want her, all of her. She's mine, my wife, my mate.

All of my senses become ultra sensitive. Her scent, her softness, the sound of her moans entice me to explore her, to get to know her better. She gently pushes me back onto the bed, her hands exploring my body, rubbing over my muscles and moving lower and lower. She moans as her hand moves down and touches my cock. I nearly exploded on her, my body taking over.

My hand explores her body, her curves. We kiss again, our lips smashing together magically. I sniff her neck, the aroma driving me to kiss and lick her skin, moving ever downward. The mounds on the front of her chest are particularly curious. One lick of my tongue and the nipple hardens. My lips cover them, tongue licking, and she moans, her hands moving up to my head, rubbing my horns. It brings a tingle down my neck and straight to my cock. I'm tingling all over, the desire to take her overcomes me. I pant, wanting her, needing her, hungering for her.

CHAPTER 6

Agnes

What is happening? I'm swept away by his mouth, his lips, his tongue. He groans, needing me, his hands groping, exploring. It's as if our drinks were spiked and the potion is working on us.

"You smell delicious." His nose moves down my belly and to the area right above my pubic bone. I groan and giggle at the same time.

Electrical streaks flash from my mid-section throughout my body. My senses are sizzling with each kiss, each sniff, each flick of his wonderful tongue. Suddenly, I'm the center of his universe and the only thing that matters is the two of us.

My body relaxes back and I open my legs, giving him what he wants. He groans as he licks and kisses. His cock stands firm, obviously I turn him on.

I lose control under the licking, he strikes right up my valley, touching me where even I haven't gone. The room dims and bright colors form in the periphery as the pleasure overtakes me. His tongue swirls over my clit, delicious, determined, absolutely unadulterated. Never have I experienced such levels of ecstasy in my life. I grab hold of his horns and hang on as I leap from the ledge and let go. My body shakes as the orgasm takes hold. His tongue masterfully swirls, bearing down, not leaving me without full completion.

I gasp and moan, my body rolling through the waves of pleasure that take hold of me. My hands hold his horns to me until I finish and can't take another swipe of his tongue. Shoving back, I push him away and scoot up on the bed and collapse, panting for air feeling completely satisfied.

Vozak lifts, his face glistening from my pleasure. He grabs my legs as he slides to the floor and stands at the edge of the bed.

"My turn," he growls.

I scoot to the edge of the bed and wrap my legs around his waist. He pulls me up and my legs fall to the side. His face is inches from mine, so close I smell myself on him and it turns me on. Our lips smash together, the urgency in the passion accelerates his moans, his moves. He desperately wants me, needs me.

He pulls my feet to his waist, and I wrap my legs around him. Taking his huge cock into his hand he rubs it through my slickness swirling over my sensitive clit. My back arches as he penetrates through my little opening. I'm a virgin so it's very tight, stretching, tearing, ripping.

"Oh, ouch!" I cry but I don't want him stopping. I grab his hips and keep him to me.

"I'm hurting you. It feels so good though. You're so tight."

I suck in a deep breath. "Yes, it hurts because I'm a virgin and you're huge. But keep going. Obviously, it works for minotaurs and humans."

He rocks into me, his cock stretching me with each thrust forward. Oddly, as he moves, the ripping sensation disappears and an incredible pleasure replaces it. Vozak moves faster, his face skewing with the pleasure he's feeling, he can't help but pound into me. All things fade except for what we're doing.

Suddenly, my pelvis explodes for a second time, the ecstasy rocking through my pelvis as I arch my back and moan out of control. A second later, he pounds into me furiously, unable to stop himself. We rock through the waves of pleasure together, until I collapse back from sheer exhaustion. He finishes and pulls out, staggering backward, catching his breath.

"Are you okay, Agnes? I didn't hurt you, did I?" He comes to me, crawling onto the bed and gathers me in his arms.

"My beautiful wife, you have made me a very happy minotaur. I never realized how compatible we were. I'm glad I didn't break you, my fragile little mate." He kisses my head in a tender moment.

I curl into his side, my body still trembling with the remnants of our time together. I'm sore, lethargic, euphoric, and completely satisfied. Lying sideways on the bed, we fall asleep in each other's arms, resting contentedly all night.

The sunlight streams through the window as I stir. He's sleeping soundly, his breathing deep and even. I gaze upon his face, memorizing every detail. Minotaurs are different yet very similar. The obvious difference is the horns. I lightly touch them, and he rouses, his eyes opening to small slits, and he gazes at me.

"Good morning, husband," I say with a smile.

His arm draws me to him, our lips touch in a sweet kiss.

"Did you sleep well?" He yawns.

"I did, even though we slept sideways," I say with a giggle.

He kisses my forehead and rises. "We best get on the road so we can make it home at a decent hour."

And just like that, our honeymoon is over. He hops into the bathroom, leaving me to rise, dress, and pack.

Things are better between us, different. He's still quiet as we ride toward the Taurus Territory. Once in a while, he gazes my way with a smile. His hand slides across the bench seat of the truck and grabs mine. I scoot over because I want to be next to him. My arm curls around his, and my head rests on his strong-muscled shoulders.

"Are you happy with me, Vozak?" I ask, more as a means to have a conversation than an actual question.

He laughs. "Of course. Do you not remember last night? We mated very successfully. The honeymoon night is complete. We will arrive at our ranch and I will show you around directly."

I bounce on the seat beside him. "Can we visit Auryn and Vrakius first? I really want to see my sister first."

"We will visit them after we arrive home and take care of matters there."

CHAPTER 7

*V*ozak

The scent of my new wife sticks with me. I have a hard time concentrating on the road and the coming tasks once we arrive home. If I had my way, I'd pull to the side and take her again, and again. My body rages with desire, but I harmed her last night, as evident by the blood on me this morning. I cannot hurt her. She needs time to heal.

"Okay. We take care of matters. You'll have to teach me. All I know is living in a city colony in a tiny apartment. I've never lived on open land or know how to work on a ranch."

"Mmph. You'll catch on. I suspect Auryn will aid in your training. You're the keeper of the home."

She slips her arm out of mine. "I want to help on the ranch." She reaches for a drink we got at the last stop.

"You will. Auryn sews and cooks and takes care of the baby. She does some of the gardening. Vrakius and I take care of the livestock and the larger crops. The boarius requires some hands-on, too big for you slight humans. They have become a greater asset than the cattle we have." I wince because I don't like raising cattle. It's too close to our bovine ancestry, though we walk on two legs and are more intelligent, it's like we're killing our cousins.

"Here we are in Taurus Territory." We cross over the border, the minotaur territory stretching before us.

"Oh! It's so dry here. And flat, and wow, look at the animals."

I laugh at her description of Taurus Territory. She bounces over to the window to watch all the ranches as we drive. A caravan of South-Taupis drives by fast, and my hair stands on end. What are they doing here?

We arrive at the ranch after two hours of driving through the territory. Agnes looks around wide-eyed at the land stretching before her, taking in the fullness of the ranch. She immediately runs to the fence where the boarius gathers and squeals.

"Delightful. They look like pigs on steroids. Look at those long snouts."

I laugh at her enthusiasm. "Come on, Agnes. See the house."

The ranch home has three bedrooms, ready to fill with children. When I first came to Alia Terra, I resented the large home Vrakius had for me. Now I am hopeful to fill it with children with my new wife.

Her mouth stays agape as I take her through the kitchen. The shiny stone countertops gleam with the waning light of the day. A large gas stove, refrigerator, and freezer stand at one end, while at the other are counters, cabinets, and drawers. She opens the cabinets and takes out a ceramic plate and smiles.

"I love it." She turns to me, her face alight in a brilliant smile.

"Come on. This is the sitting room." Two sofas covered in patchwork quilts face each other over a giant round carved squatting table. The fireplace sits at one end, and the dining room is at the other.

"So much room. Our tiny library apartment back east barely fit one sofa." She sits on the sofa and bounces.

"Come on, see the bedrooms."

"How many?"

The first two are the spare rooms. Each one has a bed covered in a quilt and a chest of drawers. "Three."

"Three?" She follows me into the largest of the bedrooms, ours. Auryn came in and made the bed, adding sheets with embroidered edges and a lovely quilt in soft colors. For a romantic ambience, she said.

"Wow. This is nice."

"And we have a large bathroom."

"A claw foot tub! Oh wow! I've seen pictures of them in the old magazines. How neat!" She runs to it and steps inside and slips down, pretending like she's bathing. The thought of her naked makes my cock grow hard.

I reach for my new wife and pull her to me. The rest of the ranch can wait. We haven't been together since last night. "How are you?"

"I'm fine." She looks at me like I asked the silliest question.

"I mean after last night. You bled some when we mated."

Her face turns a bright pink. "It's normal, I'm fine."

I pull her to me, lowering my face to hers and planting a kiss on her lips. "Are you okay to do it again?" I press my urgency against her and she giggles.

"I'm fine, husband. But you haven't shown me the ranch. Or we haven't seen my sister yet."

I pull her to the bedroom again, my hands are on her clothes, tugging and pulling to free her sweet body. She giggles and helps and then turns to me, helping me out of my clothes.

We tumble to the bed, rolling onto our sides facing each other. I want to ravage her, but I hold back knowing fragile humans can't take that. She pulls her hair to the side and I roll to my back while she hoists herself over me, on top.

"I'm glad we've found our way physically. If that's the only time I get your affection, then so be it." She leans in and our lips touch and I'm wondering what she means by that. The physical urges take over and I'm caught up in the wonder of the moment.

"Let me take you for a ride." She busts out laughing. "Sorry, I've always wanted to say that. I read it in one of those trashy romance novels."

Her small body moves over me and she grabs my cock with her sweet little hands. Hovering, she easily guides me inside. I barely fit, but she wiggles her hips until I slid all the way in.

"You really are big. Wow." Her body moves over me, squeezing as she rocks up and down. I moan and help her by grabbing her hips and moving her faster.

CHAPTER 8

Agnes

Vozak groans as I move faster over him. Leaning forward, the friction between us sparks pleasure in me.

"Wait for me." I moan, wanting to go with him, but he's too far ahead.

"What do you mean?"

"I want to come with you." I grind over him and he slows the moves.

"Yes, come with me. Wife." His eyes looked into mine, a softness in his expression. He pulls me up and sets me to the side.

"What are you doing?"

He stands on the floor and draws me to him. "I want to help you come with me."

I grab his waist and cling to him as he penetrates me again. He shoves his hand between my legs, rubbing my clit, helping me along.

Within minutes my body trembles greatly and I launch into the orgasm. He joins me seconds later, thrusting into me fast, our bodies trembling through the throes of pleasure.

He finishes and I collapse back onto the bed, hoping he'll join me. He laughs and turns around, redressing.

"Well? You want to see the ranch?"

I want a moment of tenderness. Maybe a kiss, but my husband is all work and no affection, except when he's horny and wants to *mate*. I shrug and instead of sulking, I dress and follow him outside with the promise of seeing my sister soon.

The boarius outnumber all the other creatures by two to one.

"I don't eat bovine," Vozak grunts at me as we check the cattle with the long horns.

I laugh. I can't help it. Beef is a precious commodity where I'm from. We're accustomed to eating mostly vegetables grown in the surrounding farmlands. But if beef was available, they would eat it.

"Vrakius eats it. Auryn tells me how she cooks both beef and boarius."

"No bovine will be eaten in this home." Vozak looks at me with a final authoritative expression.

My brow furrows, and I don't like it. No discussion, no gentle words. He's all or nothing. What's that old saying? A bull in a china shop. Yeah, that's it. He's all gruff and domi-nating. I'm not sure I will enjoy a relationship where he's only tender with me while we're doing it. It's nothing like what I saw with Vrakius and Auryn. I'm beginning to wish I had Chelsea find me a nice Phoenix instead.

"You coming?" He stands at the door as I slip my feet into the sneakers.

On one hand, I'm not entirely pleased with my new husband. But on the other hand, in a strange way, it's as if we've known each other for years, it feels that comfortable.

He smiles as I join him on the grand tour of the ranch. Out of the corner of my eye, I swear I see someone ducking behind the trees. "Do you have workers on the ranch?"

"Sometimes. Vrakius will bring in others to help on occa-sion. No one right now. Vrakius came over while I was away."

"I think I just saw someone hiding among the trees over there." I point.

Vozak grunts. "Who's there?" He stomps and runs toward the area, but whoever it was is long gone by the time he reaches the area.

After an exhaustive search, nothing comes up, and we move on. Still, my skin prickles as I look in that direction. We tour the gardens and the livestock. While he's adamant about not eating cows, he has them in one of his pastures. But he has three times as many boarius, which are very pig-like.

"Are we going to visit Auryn now?"

He sighs. "Yes."

At least Auryn provides the bright spot in my life now. Being married to Vozak is an adventure, but not the one I dreamed about having.

Auryn and Vrakius have a big dinner waiting for us when we arrive. Both of us squeal as we embrace.

"My darling baby sister finally got her minotaur." Auryn pulls hair from my face as we rear back from the hug.

"Yes." I sigh and shake my head, my eyes rolling. I can't help it, but I'm no longer impressed with this whole marriage thing. Mind-blowing sex isn't good enough to make for a happy marriage.

Auryn pulls me into her kitchen while Vozak and Vrakius discuss what's going on around the ranches. Little Dario runs up trying to say Aunt Agnes, only it comes out An Anes.

"What's going on, hon?" She opens the oven and pulls out loaves of bread which smell absolutely mouthwatering.

"Vozak is um, I don't know. Maybe not what I was expecting, especially since he's Vrakius' brother. I guess I was hoping for my happy-ever-after."

Auryn laughs. "You've read too many books, Agnes. Has he said or done anything to hurt you?"

"No. He's not hurt me. Just not what I expected. It's nothing like you described when you and Vrakius married."

"Oh honey, you need to give it time. Vrakius fell in love instantly. Not everyone does. I have friends who had to grow into it."

"He's a great lover, but he doesn't really pay any attention to me unless he's, you know." My eyes widen as I talk.

"Give it time. He's fresh from Tariat and doesn't know the human ways as well as those who have been here longer."

"What's going on in here?" Vrakius walks in carrying Dario and smiles at us.

"Nothing but sister talk, dearest," Auryn says. She and Vrakius have such a sweet and loving relationship. He walks to her and kisses her on the cheek.

Vozak saunters inside and takes a seat at the table. He's reading over some sort of document written in their language. He looks up at me as he grabs a pear and takes a bite.

"Seems you may be right in seeing someone on the ranch. Rumors of bandits coming around and stealing livestock. We may have a war on our hands."

CHAPTER 9

*V*ozak

My mate just gawks at me as I eat the pear. "Why aren't you going out there and doing something about it then?"

"I'm sure our presence earlier scared them off. But don't worry, there's an all-out war on them."

"South Taupas?" Auryn sets the freshly sliced bread on the table.

"Yeah, and probably some Darthcol pirates. Seems they have a system working to our south, not in the same area we settled earlier."

"It feels like we can never relax around here." Auryn's brow furrows as she scoops up Dario.

"What are we going to do?" Agnes puts her hand on my hip, showing I mean business.

"We? You are a fragile human. You will stay out of our way while we deal with these bandits." My mate thinks she can handle the likes of the bandits, and she's dead wrong.

Auryn shoots me a disapproving look. I take my place by Agnes at the table as we prepare for the meal. Agnes dominates the conversation as they talk about ranch life and what she'll do on ours.

"You'll keep the home, cook, garden, and give birth to my babies." I say it, hoping she'll heed it.

"I'm not your prisoner. I thought being married would mean I'd have the freedom to go outside and do things. Not the same things I did back home." Agnes glares at me. Then she looks at Auryn. "See what I mean?" She rises and leaves the table.

"I got this." Vrakius goes after her.

Auryn steps to me and nods for the door. I follow her. She whips around on me, her hand on her hip, and a sour expression on her face.

"My little sister isn't too happy. Vozak, what have you done to her?" The accusatory tone angers me.

"I've done nothing to hurt her, if that's what you mean. She's had a smile on her face; I know how to please a human female." My arms cross over my chest.

"Have you told her you love her?" Her head shakes.

"Love her? We just met."

"You mated, right?"

I chuckle. Sarcasm comes across nicely. "Of course, we did."

"Clearly, you and Vrakius are vastly different."

"If you are implying that I should be just like my older brother, I am sorry. I am me, not him. And if Agnes has a problem with me, then she needs to tell me, not you."

"Look, Vozak, the comparison she's making with your relationship is by what Vrakius and I have. Obviously, you aren't the same as him. I'm hoping you'll give my sister a chance. She's more than just a mate, someone to bear your children. She has hopes and dreams and wants the love story too."

I gaze at Auryn. "I don't know what a love story is or how to give one. Remember, I come from Tariat, and I only know what I've seen there between minotaurs."

"Listen, Vozak, just be her friend. Include her in your day. Let her be your partner, and she'll find her way into your life. That's what she wants more than anything else."

I sit on the stool, feeling defeated. "I guess I don't know how to do that."

Auryn, always sweet, pats my shoulders. "Just pretend Agnes is like Vrakius in the respect that you talk with him and work with him. I know she can't lift heavy bales of hay, but she's resourceful. I promise if you do this, she'll be your most loyal friend. And bonus, she's your wife and lover."

"Lover. It's just called mate on Tariat."

"This is Alia Terra. Humans have lovers, those who extend their affections beyond the mating. She needs to learn patience with you. It's a process. And she's filled her head with romance novels from our old library back home."

I nod. "Yes, I hear you, and I will try. Honesty, I fully believe Agnes is my one. I have a lot of Tariat in me, and the minotaur way is vastly different there than it is here. I keep reminding myself she's a fragile human and not a hearty female minotaur. She and I are both figuring this out."

"Just figure it out together. Let her work by your side, and you help with the domestic duties. There was a time women played larger roles in everything before the fall. We were reduced to the edges of society when the aliens landed."

"We're all trying together. I better get back to my lovely mate."

"That's what I'm talking about." Auryn smiles warmly as I walk out of the kitchen to find her.

I grab Agnes' hand, and she looks up at me surprised. "We should get back home. It's getting late, and we've had a couple of busy days. Tomorrow I will show you how to do tasks on the ranch with me."

"Really?" Her face stretches into a bright smile, beautifully.

My heart truly beats happier with her by my side. I need to learn how to express it. I want her to be happy.

"What changed?" She asks as we walk back to our home.

"Changed? Nothing. Well, Auryn made me realize what's important. I'm sorry if I made you think I don't like having you around. I know we just met two days ago, but truly you are my mate."

She pauses and turns to me. "Do you mean that?"

The moon rises, casting silvery light reflecting in her eyes. I wrap my arms around her, my body warming to her presence, and pull her close. Leaning in, I'm inches from her face. "Yes." The gap closes, and we kiss, the emotions stirring deep in my heart.

Her soft and supple body melts into mine, right under the moonlight. I could claim her right here outside. She groans, her need for me as evident as my need for her.

Leaning back, she smiles. "Let's get home and be comfortable."

"Sounds like a good plan." I scoop her up and partly run with her in my arms back to our home.

CHAPTER 10

Agnes

Something changed in Vozak after Auryn talked to him. Whatever it was, I love it. He carries me all the way back to the house like we're fevered for each other. Once inside, he grabs my hand and brings me to the bathroom where we come out of our clothes like our lives depend on it. The large tub holds both of us standing under the streaming shower with the curtain pulled all the way around. It's cozy and erotic with his buff naked body standing in front of me.

"Here, I will wash you. This gives me an opportunity to get to know you better." He takes the large sponge and rubs the soap cake over it.

I turn around and stretch giving him access to all of me. He slowly rubs the sponge over my body, taking time, exploring and getting to know me better. I giggle when he gets to my armpits.

"Oh really? You like this, huh?"

I squeal as he moves his soapy fingers over my folds and sparks the passion boiling in my body. I take hold of the sponge and give him a round of cleaning. He's so big I can't reach everything so he kneels so I can soap him everywhere.

Slowly, I rub over his muscles, and his body, moving ever downward. "Stand." He obeys my command and I finish by scrubbing every square inch of him. He's far larger than any human male I've read about. No wonder I bled after the first and second times. Still, my body hums at his touch and the desire builds.

We dry quickly and before I put the towel down, he kneels before me. Smiling, he leans in, his face moving between my legs. I stumble back and perch on the edge of the tub, opening my legs giving him greater access.

Leaning in, he gently kisses me there. I moan, the blood flowing to my pelvis. Slowly and softly he kisses and licks and nibbles through my soft warm folds.

"You smell so wonderful. Amazing. I can't get enough."

My body soars at his words, his kisses sending me over the edge. I cling to his head, holding him in place while I rock through the waves of pleasure coursing through my body. I shove him back as I finish. He doesn't waste a moment when he scoops me up and carries me to the bedroom.

I lie back and he crawls up to me, partially hovering but not squishing me. His large hand comes to my face, brushing my damp hair from my eyes. "Agnes, do you love me?"

I can't help but laugh at the question. "You are my husband, of course I do."

"I'm trying to learn what love is. What lovers are."

Now, I'm curious. My hand reaches for his face, stroking his chiseled jaw. "Lovers are two people who love each other and who make love, or as you put it, mate. But making love isn't always about mating, or trying to make a baby. It's doing it because you enjoy each other. See?"

"I love you, Vozak. I don't know why, but I know I do." Smiling, my arms encircle me.

"From what Auryn says about love, then I feel the same way."

I sit up and roll him to the bed and hover over him, my face nearly touching his nose. "Then say it."

"Say what?" He gazes into my eyes, pulling me into his realm, under his spell. I am at home with him, even though we had a rough start.

"If you love me too, say it."

"I love you too."

I giggle. It's not said with the loving inflections yet, but maybe in due time. Those darn romance novels really skewed my perception of marriage. None of the books were about aliens marrying humans.

"I love you, I want you, I am glad you are my wife." Smart minotaur.

I lift my body over him, hoisting my middle above his giant swollen cock. He stretches into me, my tight tunnel squeezing around. It's getting easier, but he's so big I verge on pain as I sit with him fully inside me.

He helps me lift over him. My hips move as I go up and down with his help. He groans each time I come down. I suck in a deep breath, my body tipping into the direction of another pelvic explosion. We grind against each other until my body topples and I'm shaking through the throes of a second orgasm.

Vozak joins me moments later, and we rock through the unrelenting waves of pleasure until both of us finish. Only then do I collapse on top of him as his strong arms encircle me. We lie quietly catching our breath and basking in the afterglow of lovemaking.

I roll to the side and curl into him. He draws me to him, his other hand rubbing circles over my shoulder. "Are you happy, Agnes?"

My brow furrows as I giggle. "What kind of question is that?"

"I realize I need to make making you happy as one of my top priorities."

I rise on my elbow. "No, you don't. Happiness is something we choose, it's not something you have to work at. Because if you have to work at it, then it's not real. Does that make sense?"

He looks up, thinking. "Yeah, it does. How about tomorrow I teach you how to run the ranch. Maybe you can teach me how to read those books you love so much."

"Really?" This is news. "I love my books, but they're back home."

"There's bound to be books in these areas too. If not, we'll search for the old books."

"I would like that very much."

"Just like I'll enjoy showing you the ranch and teaching you how to take care of the livestock and garden."

We fall asleep in each other's arms, dreaming about our new life together.

CHAPTER 11

*V*ozak

Agnes flips the strips of boarius in the skillet, the eggs whipped and ready to cook. She baked a loaf of fresh minotaur bread, the ingredients came from Auryn complete with instructions. Even the fresh butter and blackberry jam Auryn made for us is on the table ready to consume.

"I hope you like this. Auryn said boarius is very much like pork. The salt-cured strips are like bacon, and smell similar. But it tastes a little different."

Outside, she keeps up with me as I take her around checking the barns and the livestock. Then at the garden, she kneels checking the root vegetables.

"I went with my mother to the community garden back home."

"You're quite capable of doing this."

For a couple of weeks, we slip into a routine. We work together with every ranch task, and she keeps up in all of it. She teaches me how to cook human foods and I teach her the minotaur foods.

One month of marriage comes with a celebration. Agnes and I take a trip south to pick up supplies for the ranch, staying overnight along the way at a small inn.

"Vozak, I didn't want to say anything until I knew for sure, but I don't like keeping things from you."

I hold her tighter, the day's work of gathering supplies for the ranch left us exhausted and we ate an early dinner and came to the inn for a good night's rest. Her words worry me. "No, don't keep things from me. Are you ill?"

She shakes her head and giggles. "No, my sweet bull man, I'm not ill." Rolling to me, her body rests on mine as my body warms and my loins stand at attention. "But I think I might be pregnant."

Excitement rushes through me. "Already?"

She sits up fully and turns to me. "Well, yeah. It only takes once. And we've been together practically every night."

"Your blood cycle showed up a week after we married." It was the longest five days waiting for her to finish.

"I'm late, like a week late. And I'm ravenously hungry and at the same time, certain foods make me want to hurl."

I laugh. "Yesterday you refused the meat pie at lunch."

She turns and makes a gagging noise. "Sorry, but the thought of eating meat is just gross."

"You may very well be pregnant."

"Are you happy?"

A rumble of laughter rolls through my body. Holding my mate who just told me she might be pregnant makes me the happiest minotaur on Alia Terra. "Yes! But this will change things around the ranch."

"What do you mean?" Her brow furrows.

"I mean, I'm not having my pregnant wife out there doing hard labor. I want you and the baby safe and healthy."

"I'm not so fragile that I can't put in a good day's work. Maybe I shouldn't lift heavy things, but I can certainly help feed and water the animals and weed and water the garden. And when the time comes, I can help harvest the vegetables."

"Okay, okay. All I ask is that if you need a break, you take a break. And if you need to stick close to the house, you can."

"I know, love."

Her naked body moves on top of me. With her potentially being pregnant, I don't want to risk hurting her by being in control. Sweet love flows between us as she climbs on me, and with my help, she gingerly lowers her tight, soft tunnel over my rock-hard cock. I nearly lose control, but with her on top, she's safer. Together we rush through the layers of pleasure, her body rocking first as she comes and then me. I hold her hips, helping her move until I drain my cock.

She snuggles into my arms, falling asleep with a satisfied smile on her beautiful face. I gaze upon her for a long time, thankful she's my DNA match. A baby will bring us closer, and seal our fate.

We head back home the next day and Agnes makes an appointment with the minotaur healer who is also married to a human midwife. It's a perfect match, and they moved into our area right after I arrived on Alia Terra.

Sara and Janos have full schedules with all the minotaurs having pregnant mates. There's a boom of half-human, half-minotaur babies increasing Taurus Terra. They will see her later in the week.

"I'll talk to Auryn." My bright-eyed mate smiles at me, the excitement of a possible pregnancy certainly becomes her.

"First, let's tend the livestock and check the garden. Only if you're up to it?" I don't want to flex my domination over her, but I will if I think she's hurting from doing too much ranch work.

Agnes wanders into the garden carrying a basket to harvest cucumbers and cherry tomatoes. I move over to the cattle range and take care of fencing repairs. Turning to look at her as I walk away, my heart swells seeing my mate, potentially pregnant, happily kneeling and plucking the cucumbers from the vines.

The overcast skies keep the glare at bay, a soft breeze breaking the heat that tends to swelter by mid-afternoon. Out of my periphery, I spy something moving in the distance. For a split second, I thought I heard Agnes crying for help. But listening, I hear nothing and shake my head. Thoughts of Agnes thinking she saw something when she first arrived dart through my mind. I quickly rush back to the garden.

"Agnes?" Nothing but the breeze answers and the lowing of the cattle behind me. The sun slips in the west, casting long shadows. "Agnes?"

A glance at the garden and I see it's empty. She must have gone back to the house. I turn, but something catches my eye in the tomatoes. A basket, her basket, which she would not have left if it were filled with vegetables. Icy fear claws down my spine when I arrive at the basket and see it's partially turned over, cucumbers and cherry tomatoes spilled out all over the ground.

CHAPTER 12

*A*gnes

I couldn't wait to see Janos and Sara to find out if I'm pregnant. Tonight, I'll venture over to Auryn's and talk with her about it. We've both been busy. I enjoy working outside. Back home on the eastern seaboard, the homes and apartments in our little community were so close, there was nothing but concrete outside. The community garden was the only spot of ground and it was tiny. Out here on the ranch, the land stretches as far as the eyes can see, and we can't even see our neighbors. It's pastures full of animals and the garden that's five times bigger than the community back at my parents' home.

The basket filled halfway with cucumbers. I move to the tomatoes because I'm craving a salad. Surely, I'm pregnant. Happiness flows over me as I kneel at the tomato plants. I love growing our food and raising our meat. Vozak is talking about getting some chickens.

Suddenly, something goes over my head and pulls me back. I start to scream. "Help!" A hand goes over my mouth, dragging me backward. Struggling does no good, they have a tight grip and pull me away. When I try to run, they roughly pull me along, causing me to stumble. For fear of hurting myself and my baby, I don't fight too hard.

I can't talk, I can't run. Someone lifts me, throwing me over a shoulder. My arms are free, and I beat whoever it is on the back. They slam me down, and my head hits something hard. Blackness takes over as I pass out.

Jostling around, I wake up still with the hood over my face and hear the sound of a slight unrecognizable hum. I move and brace myself for the impending hit, but nothing comes. My hand reaches up and pulls the hood from my face. I'm lying on a pad on the floor of a metallic room. Oh no! I'm nowhere near the ranch, and I fear I'm far from home by now. How long was I out?

My legs wobble as I stand, the pounding in my head throbs with my heartbeat. Reaching up, I feel a lump on the side of my head where they must have hit me when I passed out.

Two doors are adjacent. I try one and realize it's a bathroom with a metal toilet and a tiny sink. I've never seen this type of thing before. Since it's a bathroom, I take advantage. Pregnancy causes one to pee a lot. I really need to talk to Auryn. But first, I need to ditch this place.

The other door opens, and it's a hall winding around in a circle. Chattering comes from the double door, the place lurches, and I topple over, yelling as I fall.

"Oh!"

They come through the doors, the same ones I saw on the ranch when I first arrived at Taurus Terra. The South Taupas, the aliens from the southern territory. They glare at me, their furry brows furrow.

I jump up and back away quickly, my hands up.

"No! Leave me alone, let me leave."

He laughs. "Stupid human. Try to leave, you'll die."

"Let me go! Why did you grab me?" Tears stain my eyes.

"We have a reason."

"I'm leaving." I march away, and again, the place lurches, and I fall. "What in the world?"

The South Taupas grabs me and pulls me along into the room through the double doors. With utter horror, I see we're in a spaceship and flying in outer space. The window shows black with stars.

"You've abducted me in a spaceship? Where are you taking me?"

"We're in Terra's realm. You're our bargaining chip. We want something, and the minotaurs have it."

"Please," I cry. The hairy Taupas keeps hold of me, not letting go.

"Sit," he commands. I sit, and they belt me into the chair. "Tell us how much land your minotaur has in his possession."

"I don't know. He's not going to hand over his land. And the minotaurs claimed the land long ago. It's theirs. Don't you have your territory south of it?"

"It's a dry desert. We need land with rich soil, land that will help us grow crops and have animals like you have."

Anger bubbles inside me. "The land is not for Vozak to give away. Nor is it for you to capture. Using me as a pawn to get the land won't work." I'm defiant enough to play the game with them. One thing I know about the minotaurs is they are fiercely loyal to their family. My husband will do whatever it takes to get me back.

"You are not going back to Terra until we get what we want."

"Why don't you find other land to claim? Why minotaur territory?"

"It's similar to our home planet Tapania."

"What about the land to the west of Taurus Terra?" I really wasn't sure about the terrain there, but I heard it was a desert there too."

"All the land in Alia Terra is claimed by others. We arrived too late for the choice land."

I glare at them. "You can't just demand Taurus Territority. There are other parts of the world you can find. Go elsewhere. Take me home, or the minotaurs will declare war on you." I am not sure of the truth of that, but it sounded good, threatening.

"We will have that land. Or you will be our slave." The leader unbelted me from the chair and led me around the circular hall to a room that had medical devices. The South Taupas steps to me with a needle. Oh no! Now, I put up a fight. I refuse to let them harm me.

"Get away from me." I take a swing, and from behind, something pierces me in the back of my neck, and the world fades once again.

CHAPTER 13

Vozak

I burst into the house, hoping she got sick and rushed home instead of disappearing. "Agnes? Agnes?" The house is eerily quiet. A quick search, and I'm confident she's not here. Back outside, I holler for her over and over and search every bit of the land.

"Vrakius, Agnes has disappeared." I left a message on his comm. If he's out working on his newfound interest, horses, he's not listening for his comm. I check the house again and scour the garden, looking for clues. Sure enough, there are footprints in the surrounding area, at least eight pairs of different-sized shoe prints along the clods of dirt lining the garden.

My heart pounds hard, she's nowhere near here. My wife, my mate, is gone. The word around the area says there are bandits, the South Taupas, who are sniffing around and wanting our land.

I turn to head back to the barn and gather my weapons. I will hunt every single bandit and chop off their heads until they give Agnes back to me. Auryn, Dario, and Vrakius run to me as they received the message.

"We came right over." Vrakius lifts Dario, carrying him as he jogs to me.

"We came out this morning. I left her with the basket to harvest cucumbers and tomatoes while I took care of fence repairs for the livestock. I came back afterward, and she was nowhere, her basket and the vegetables on the ground. I found eight sets of footprints in the dirt clods at the edge of the garden.

"Oh no! Agnes!" Auryn cries as she catches up with Vrakius.

"Bandits." Vrakius nods. "We'll gather our sentinels. She can't have gotten far."

Tears fill Auryn's eyes. "I saw a small ship take off earlier."

Anger flows through my veins. "I will kill the entire lot of them." I shove my dagger into the sheath and grab the sword. South Taupas carry blasters, which are against the Taurus Terra law.

"Brother, you're not in this alone. I've sent out a call for help with the Taurus Sentinels. They're gathering and coming here. I suspect this will open war with the South Taupas."

I stomp away and pile into the truck. Vrakius talks with Auryn, who grabs Dario and nods.

"They're staying at your house in case Agnes comes back."

We drive the truck up the road, meeting the Taurus Sentinels and pull up beside them in their big-wheeled vehicles.

"Bandits were seen all around yesterday. They are encamped just south of here on the border." Abearon nods as I let me lead the pack. It's my wife at stake here.

My fingers white-knuckle the steering wheel. "If they harm her, I'll kill all of them."

"Calm, brother. It's more than likely a kidnapping to use against us for what they want, part of our land."

I turn to my brother, my brow furrowed. "We won't give them what they want, and we'll take back what they've stolen." South Taupas come in wanting what they didn't rightfully gain, and using warfare methods of obtaining it. The place has never fully been at peace from their shenanigans.

We pass the airfield from which their ships take off and land. They come and go to the mothership flying above this planet often, probably kidnapping others for their gain. Abearon marches forth with me on his heels. Before Abearon says a word, I draw my dagger and grab the South Taupas by the neck, threatening to spill his blood everywhere. His goons rush in to stop me, and Abearon steps between us.

"Peace, Vozak. We don't know what happened yet." Abearon tries his fairness actions first.

My hands balled into fists. "I want my wife back."

"How dare you come at me with such accusations. What is the problem?" The South Taupas growl at us, his furry brow knit as one above his beady eyes.

"My wife disappeared. Grabbed right from our garden. Eight sets of footprints, and your people were seen in the area just prior."

The South Taupas blinks at me, his mouth twitching.

"We don't want a war on our hands. Your people are trespassing on our land. I understand you want better soil, but our land is not yours." Abearon tries to talk, but the South Taupas holds up a finger and disappears. I take off after him, but Abearon and two others of the Taurus Sentinels grab me and hold me back.

"Let go. They have Agnes."

"It seems your female isn't here on the planet any longer. She's safe and will be returned if you will give up one third of your land for us."

"We're not here to bargain. The land is ours; we staked a claim on it years ago. Just like all the other aliens on Alia Terra, the land is ours. You can find unclaimed land to have like you've found south of us. This is not yours to have. It's full minotaur territory. You need to find your own Taupas territory."

"Enough!" I wave my fist in the air. "I want my wife back, then we'll deal with the land issues."

"I am Toraaj. I am the leader here. The human female is on the mothership until the land issues are to our satisfaction."

I lunge for Toraaj; my hands go around his neck. Two more Taupas swoop in and pull me back. Toraaj coughs and backs away from me. Vrakius grabs my arm and pulls me close.

"Careful, Vozak. Keep calm so they won't hurt Agnes."

I growl and come out of his grip. Reasoning isn't a part of my personality when someone I love is in trouble.

"You harm me, we harm her. If anything happens to me or any of us here, she will be the first to the space plank walk."

My blood freezes. My Agnes is up there, held captive against her will, and no doubt scared.

CHAPTER 14

*A*gnes

The cold metal room on the ship provides little comfort. My thoughts race back to feeling the prick on the back of my neck. What did they do to me? A small bandage is on my arm. I can only guess they drew blood.

Suddenly, the door bursts open, and the same Taupas strides in, glaring at me. He jabbers something in his own language.

My head shakes. "What?" My stomach rumbles, and hunger pains fog my thinking.

"You are with child. We were hoping you could carry one of ours to prove we can order wives from the marriage temple."

It's like a punch in the gut as I protectively place my hands over my belly. Vozak's baby grows in me, and it's a dream come true, except the nightmare of being on an alien ship is very real.

"Then you should bring me back to my husband. Why don't you seek help from the marriage temple? I'm sure they'll work with you if you do it legally. Kidnapping me isn't going to help you, though."

"We have a tea you can drink that will help you pass the baby. Then you can help us. Unless we try implanting one of ours during your gestation. It's risky; you could miscarry that baby anyway."

"No! I'd rather die than carry your evil spawn." I back away to the far wall, which isn't very far. The cold metal is a perfect setting for this nightmare.

"We'll see about that." He turns and leaves the room, locking the door behind him.

No! I can't allow this to happen. I need to figure out how to escape this room and hide somewhere. And then what? It's not like I can find the exit and leave the ship. I'm in space and stuck.

"Get up, follow me."

My head shakes rapidly. "No way!"

"Get up!" He growls and advances on me. Oh no! I don't want my baby harmed, so I don't fight. Reluctantly, I stand and meet him, and he places a firm hand on my upper arm.

"Stop it! You're hurting me! I won't fight."

He drags me along the circle hall, and I spy a room with weapon racks, the door open. Fear runs through my veins like icicles, but then a plan formulates. We end up at a dining hall with a long table and stools bolted to the floor. He shoves me onto a stool, and someone brings a tray with some sort of slop in a bowl and a jug of drink.

"Abortion tea?" I look up at him, and though I'm hungry, I'm scared to eat or drink.

"No. I told you, we'll try to save your baby by implanting a new one once we harvest your eggs."

I never heard of such a thing, and I shake my head. My stomach violently growls, the food, though not too appetizing, may give my baby the nourishment it needs.

The grainy cereal tastes nutty and oily. Not bad, but also not something I'd choose on purpose. I'm thirsty and slowly lift the jug, which turns out to be water. I eat cereal, scrape the bowl clean, and drink all the water.

"Come." The gruff Taupas doesn't give me a single second to sit and relax in a room other than the metal room.

"Did I sleep all night?"

"You were out for the night, yes."

I nod. Poor Vozak must be horrified with worry. "What will happen with me?"

"Unless your minotaur family comes forth with our demands, we'll try to impregnate you with our seed."

The thought makes my stomach roll. I can't allow that to happen. Think, Agnes, think. We pass the weapon room again. If I could get a weapon... He shoves me into my little metal room with the pad on the floor and shuts the door without another word.

I press my ear to the door, listening. The hall sounds quiet. The door doesn't budge though. Checking the bathroom, I find nothing. Whoever cleans this ship does a good job. Vozak must know about me by now, especially if it's been a whole day. I lost track of time being in this tiny metal room. At least I can drink water from the tiny sink. Moments tick by incredibly slowly. These people must not eat several times a day. I'm ravenously hungry again, and yet no Taupas brings me food or escorts me to the dining room. Lying on the pad, I fall asleep and wake up to what feels like hours later, my belly growling furiously now.

My fist pounds the door. "Hey! Anyone out there? Hello?"

No one answers. The metal door slides open and shut, and I try to pry at it, hoping it will come open. Surely, it has a failsafe to open in case something goes awry with the ship. Just in case, I feel along the edges on the top and high on the right edge, there are a small series of buttons. It's a sequence it's looking for as I press the buttons, a buzzing sound emits from the wall where the mechanism is.

"Come on, open."

Something happens as I press the buttons, and I hit the correct sequence, and the door slides open quietly. No one is in the hall, and the lights are dim. Maybe it's night right now? I have no way of knowing the correct time. Stowing down the hall, I come to the weapons room and enter. The dim light buzzes as if the ship is on auxiliary power. Two blasters sit in an indentation on a table, and I pick up each one. Flicking the switch, it powers up, and the trigger glows. Too easy. I turn it off and shove each one into a fabric belt tied around my waist. My next goal is to find a place to hide and figure out how to get back home.

CHAPTER 15

$\mathcal{V}$ozak

"This is absurd. My wife is up there, and we're sitting down negotiating about land. I say we take out the entire encampment." My patience is gone.

Vrakius leans in. "I know. Deleon has tracked their mothership; he just sent word. A rescue mission is in the works for going up there and bringing Agnes back. They suspect a few others are missing and up there as well."

I push back from the table. The Taupas haven't arrived yet. "What are we waiting for?"

"Brother, we can't leave. They want to negotiate with you."

"No. I want to get my wife back. I'm heading to Deleon and will fly there to save my mate. No one can stop me. I'll kill these here if I stay."

Vrakius nods. "I understand. I'd be the same way if it were Auryn or Dario."

"Then let's go."

"You go, I'll stay here and negotiate."

"Do not give them our land. They don't deserve it. Once Agnes is back, I plan to take care of their pesky presence here."

"Just go. Leave it to us."

"Deleon, when do we leave?"

"Vozak? We're firing the engines now in the Taurus Pod."

"Wait for me. I'm heading that way now. I want to go; I'll kill every one of the Taupas here if I stay." I drive the old truck as fast as I can up the dusty road toward the Taurus Airfield.

In what should have taken an hour and a half takes only forty-five minutes, and I'm pulling into the airfield, spraying rock and dust behind me.

"Vozak, we almost took off without you. Vrakius called and told us to wait; you mean business."

"Yes, I mean business. My wife is up there. The Taupas think they can take her and give her back in exchange for the land they want. I'll burn every structure down they erect and kill them with my bare hands before I let them take a single dirt clod from my land, let alone my wife." Anger releases from my body; I shake with resolve.

"We'll rescue Agnes. Then we'll deal with their demands. It's unseemly to go about it this way."

"Unseemly. Nothing they do is right."

I take a seat beside him. Two others pile in behind me.

"Vozak, don't worry, we'll bring Agnes back." Mardol is one of the best Taurus Sentinels on Alia Terra. He's known for his mercenary tactics.

"I want her back unharmed. She may be pregnant." I slump in the chair. We didn't know for sure, but my heart tells me yes, she is.

"Wonderful news, Vozak." Deleon counts down our lift-off.

"Wonderful if they haven't harmed her or the baby." My hands flex into fists. I want to hit someone, pummel them into a lifeless form.

"Have faith we will rescue her. They know if she's harmed, we don't do a thing in giving in to their demands." Lozi says. He is the co-pilot, but his kindness toward me has allowed me to sit in his seat. I can copilot too, though my chosen job is rancher and not pilot or sentinel.

We soar into the sky, the small pod shaking as it burns through the atmosphere, and within half an hour, we're free and flying in stealth toward the Taupas mothership, the Integer. Nothing hails us as we approach. The belly has landing stations, and a couple are open. We land inside one, and the door seals, shutting us in. It's the type that accommodates multiple small ships and pods, thankfully. When the door opens, the alarms screech, intruder.

Mardol pulls a tool from his belt and slides it inside the computer panel on the wall, disabling a wire. The alert stops. He turns, his mouth straight. "That should work for a while, until their computer finds a workaround. It pays to learn the enemy's technology."

"Indeed."

The ship is eerily quiet, and no one is in the circling hall. They must have left the ship on autopilot. Deleon peeks into the bridge and holds up two fingers.

"Why are they there? Why didn't they come when the alarm went off?" I am suspicious of their quietness.

"They are wearing communication headsets. Probably the ship hadn't alerted them yet." Lozi shrugs. "We are talking about the ignorant Taupas here."

"Ignorant they may be, but they are smart enough to capture humans."

We circle around the giant hall, looking in rooms, searching for anyone aside from the two goons on the bridge.

"Split up." Deleon takes off in one direction while Mardol and Lozi head back and angle off in other directions.

I forge ahead and wander through the dining hall to another hall in the back of it. Each room I check is empty.

"Agnes?"

Something thumps to my right and back. It's the grate to the ventilation system. Bending, I see Agnes through the slats. Quickly, I tear the grate off.

"Vozak!" Her eyes fill with tears, and she's pointing two blasters at me.

"Agnes, my love!"

She cries as she crawls out of the vent. I take the blasters from her and pull her into my embrace.

"They were... they were going to kill our baby to implant another of theirs in me." She cries so hard she hiccups.

"Wait! What? Our baby? Are you sure you're pregnant?"

She nods, the tears flowing. "Yes. They knocked me out and tested me. They wanted to harvest my eggs and implant one of their babies in me to prove they can mate with humans. But they said I was pregnant and it presented a problem."

"Oh, my sweet wife. I'm here. No one will harm you, ever. Are there other humans here?"

"I don't think so. They talked about bringing more."

"We must be vigilant about protecting our families in Taurus Territory. Come, we need to get out of here before they realize we're here."

Deleon, Mardol, and Lozi meet us at the pod. The two Taupas never knew we were on board the ship, thanks to cutting the wire. Just as we enter the pod, the computer of the mothership comes back online, and the alarms blare.

"Quick!" Deleon shoves the button, and the pod seals. We buckle into our seats fast as the Integer opens the seal to let us fly free. Just as we descend from the belly, three Taupas pods approach.

CHAPTER 16

Agnes

In a flurry of shots from the Taupas pods, our Taurus Pod rolls away, narrowly avoiding the initial blows. One of the blasts strikes the pod, causing it to shudder greatly, but it manages to keep flying away. We're securely belted into our seats with shoulder straps and lap belts. The pod jostles as Deleon expertly maneuvers to evade the pursuing pods.

"One is on our tail." Deleon punches commands into the bridge panel, his focus fixed on what lies ahead.

It's my first time in space, but I can't fully appreciate the experience due to the space bandits hot on our heels.

Vozak reaches for my hand. "We'll make it back. The pod's hull is resilient and can withstand a certain amount of fire."

"It's the 'certain amount' that worries me." I let out a scream as the pod rolls once more, narrowly dodging another barrage of enemy fire.

"Deleon is an exceptional pilot trained for combat space flight." Vozak's words are meant to reassure, but my fear still simmers.

"Why are they doing this?"

"We invaded their private ship and took something from them," Mardol explains.

"Took back, you mean. I don't belong to them. We just reclaimed what was rightfully ours."

"True. They have no qualms about invading our spaces, but they turn hostile when the tables are turned." Lozi's voice comes from the navigation nest above us.

Deleon hits the mic. "SOS, Taurus Pod One to Taurus Sentinels, over."

"Commander Chieftain Wilz here. Go ahead, Taurus Pod One, over." The minotaur on the ground responds.

"We have two pods from the *Integer* on our tail, firing upon us. We've sustained one hit and require assistance. Over." Deleon executes another evasive maneuver.

My head spins dizzily from the rapid maneuvers, and the chaos of the chase gives me a pounding headache.

"We'll fly low until backup arrives." Lozi peeks over the bubble at the top of the pod.

Deleon descends rapidly, the sensation of falling triggering a wave of nausea.

"Oh no! Vozak, I think I'm going to be sick." I look to him desperately for help.

"Hold on, Agnes. Anything you need." Vozak's concern is palpable.

My body shakes violently, and I vomit, the remnants of the little water I had earlier splattering around as the pod continues to tumble.

"*Drait.*" Mardol is hit with some of the aftermath.

Vozak searches for something to clean up the mess and hands me a box in case I need it again, not for cleaning up but to hold in case I get sick once more.

"I'm so sorry. I can't handle all this spinning around."

"Don't worry, Agnes. It's either this or taking fire, and the pod can only endure so much of that." Deleon maneuvers the ship sharply, causing my stomach to churn.

Finally, Vozak finds a container and empties its contents into a drawer beneath the seat. He thrusts it toward me. Fortunately, despite the continued turbulence, I managed to keep from getting sick again. Probably because I had very little to eat on the Integer, mainly just drinking water.

"Commander Chieftain Wilz here. We are closing in with stealth mode engaged and will provide a countdown. Perform the fall reverse maneuver when instructed."

"Roger that." Deleon prepares to execute the maneuver.

"Taurus Pod One, this is Taurus Fighter coming in on your left. Taurus Bringer is approaching from your right. We have the rogue pods in our sights. Prepare to release and execute the reverse maneuver in five, four, three, two, one."

"Roger that." Deleon disengaged the thrust speed, causing the ship to drop away from the pursuing ships. He initiated the reverse maneuver, and suddenly, the four ships were positioned in front of us. In a spectacular display of fireworks, the Taurus ships unleashed a barrage of fire upon the Taupas pods, setting them ablaze in the sky before us. The resulting explosions painted the sky with a burst of colorful sparks. While visually stunning, it's a bittersweet sight as the demise of the Taupas in those pods becomes evident.

I'm not feeling well as we head back toward Alia Terra. With only a bowl of cereal and some water over the past twenty-four hours, I feel weak. The trauma of our escape has left me anxious and light-headed.

"Will there be consequences?" It's a straightforward question. Our actions resulted in their deaths, and retaliation might be a concern.

"No. We were well within our rights to defend ourselves and our property. They initiated the attack," Deleon responds, his gaze briefly turning to me.

"They violated the treaty by their actions. I suspect the Taurus Sentinels will take significant measures to ensure our safety," Lozi adds with a nod.

We descend rapidly to the ground, the landing happening much faster than I anticipated. Once we touch down, Vozak is by my side before I can even unbuckle my seatbelt.

"I'll carry you." His tone is firm, his concern for my well-being evident.

I manage a weak laugh. "I'm alright, really. Just famished."

"I'm sure Auryn will have some food ready for us." Vozak glances at his wrist comm. "Vrakius sent a message saying to come straight over."

Auryn had been just as worried about me as Vozak. This adventure has been a whirlwind, one that might linger in my thoughts for a while.

Joy fills my heart as Auryn steps outside, rushing toward me with a towel in her hand. Behind her, little Dario follows, squealing with delight at the sight of me.

"Aunt Nes!"

I scoop the young boy into my arms and embrace my sister tightly. Auryn links her arm through mine and guides us into her home.

"I've prepared a hearty beef stew, sorry Vozak." She looks back at my husband, who waves at her while shaking his head.

"It's alright. I must admit, the beef is delicious." Vozak joins me at the sink as I wash my hands and face.

"I was so terrified I might lose our baby and you."

CHAPTER 17

V ozak

Auryn gazes at us wide-eyed as she settles into her seat next to Dario, who sits between her and Vrakius.

"Did I hear correctly? You're pregnant?" She glances from Agnes to me, her surprise evident.

Agnes, visibly tired and weakened, manages a smile and nods as I ladle stew into her bowl. "They informed me about it on the *Integer*. Oh, Auryn, it was terrifying!" Agnes's voice trembles, and tears stream down her cheeks as she recalls the harrowing experience.

I'm close to tears myself; the mere thought of losing our unborn child or Agnes is overwhelming.

"They drugged me and ran tests. When I woke up in that room aboard the ship, one of them entered and told me about the pregnancy. I had a feeling, and I wanted to confirm it with Sara and Janos before sharing the news. But then they revealed their intention for me to carry their child and mentioned an abortion tea. It was horrifying. Agnes and I have longed for this child more than anything. And then they said they'd implant their baby alongside ours, possibly leading to our baby's demise. That's when I knew I had to find a way out."

I chuckle lightly. "Yeah, I found her hidden in the vents behind a grate, armed with two blasters."

"No way!" Auryn's astonishment shifts between me and Agnes.

"I had to do something. They left me in that room for what felt like an eternity. In desperation, I discovered a hidden panel of buttons and managed to decipher the sequence to open the door. I knew the location of the weapons room, so I grabbed the blasters from there. Afterward, I scoured the ship for a suitable hiding spot, and the vents seemed like the best option. I figured they wouldn't check there immediately. Honestly, I didn't have a clear plan in mind. Perhaps I would locate an escape pod and attempt to reach Alia Terra, calling for help along the way. But I had no idea how to operate it. Another thought was to eliminate them one by one and send a distress signal from the bridge."

Vrakius chuckles and shakes his head. "Had you gone that route, their allies on the planet would have retaliated."

"Well, then Vozak found me, and we narrowly escaped our lives after that intense space encounter."

"Please, eat, my love. You need sustenance," I encourage Agnes gently.

Auryn reaches across the table for Agnes's hand. "Absolutely, eat. If you're carrying a child, your body requires nourishment."

"Truth be told, I'm also anxious about staying here. What if they return?" Agnes voices her fears.

I offer a soothing back rub. "The Taurus Sentinels have stationed guards around our land. They won't dare to approach now. Plus, they will face consequences for their actions."

"I believe it's more likely that we'll fortify Taurus Alia with walls, similar to what other communities have done. There's no central governing system here; we select our territories and safeguard them as we see fit. We learn from the practices of other regions across the continent," Vrakius explains, demonstrating his attentiveness to current affairs.

"I can envision us bringing in more minotaurs to protect the walls if we pursue that route," I add, smiling at Agnes, hoping to ease her apprehensions about safety.

"I'm certain that's in the works," Vrakius confirms. "Preparations are already underway."

Auryn shares a smile with Vrakius and grasps his hand, their unspoken connection evident. While Agnes and I may not be at that point yet, I hold onto the belief that we will reach it in due time.

"We've got some news too. I recently discovered that I'm about three months pregnant with our second child." Auryn squeezes Agnes' hand again, her excitement palpable. "This means our babies will be growing up together!"

Agnes' eyes shimmer with tears, and her free hand covers her mouth. "Oh, that's so wonderful for you both! Such fantastic news! I'll feel more certain once I've seen Sara and Janos."

I embrace my wife tightly, pulling her close. "I think it's time for us to head home. You deserve a proper night's rest."

"A shower sounds wonderful too." Agnes chuckles, sharing another warm embrace with Auryn.

As we walk back home, I keep my arm securely around her shoulders. "Are you absolutely sure you won't let me carry you?" I admit, I would feel more at ease with her safely in my arms.

"No, my love. I'm not helpless. I can walk on my own. Besides, I need to confront my fears. I can't always hide behind you, can I? I'd appreciate it if you could teach me to use weapons, and I'd like to keep a couple with me at all times."

After Agnes enjoys a lengthy shower, she nestles beside me in bed. My body naturally gravitates towards her, but I resist my urges. She's been through a traumatic experience and requires tender care and rest.

We share a kiss, and I muster the strength to refrain from taking her passionately. She pouts playfully, her eyes searching mine in the soft dimness of the room. "What's the matter? Don't you desire me?"

"My beloved, I crave you more than anything in the world. However, I also understand that you've had little rest and have endured a lot. Right now, you need to unwind. We have plenty of time for passionate love later. I want you to close your eyes and dream of our promising future. I'll be right here, watching over you and our precious baby."

"If there's indeed a baby." She smiles and snuggles into my embrace.

I remain awake for hours, attuned to the sounds outside. The cattle's lowing and the boarius' grunts create a soothing backdrop as they rest. The wind dances around our home, causing the boards to creak softly. Clouds roll in, and a gentle rain commences. Despite the weather's changes, Agnes slumbers peacefully, her chest rising and falling rhythmically, a serene smile gracing her lips. She finds contentment and joy within my arms.

Eventually, I drift into slumber as well, enjoying a better night's rest than I've had in quite a while. Nothing in the world holds more significance to me than the humans sleeping soundly beside me.

CHAPTER 18

$\mathcal{A}$gnes

Sara and Janos come to visit, bringing their medical tools and test kits for a thorough examination. They're renowned experts here and live close by, which is comforting. Even Auryn relies on their expertise for her own pregnancy.

Sara places her stethoscope on my belly, her gaze focused, and then hands it to her husband, who also listens intently. His expression remains serious until he breaks into a wide smile. "Yes, I believe we're hearing a heartbeat."

Vozak's hand tightens around mine, and they pass the device to me. I strain to listen, the sound faint but unmistakable – a quick, rhythmic thump blending with the slower beat of my own heart. Relief washes over me like a tidal wave. My baby is safe. Vozak's eyes well up with tears as he hears the precious sound.

Sara's smile radiates warmth. "Congratulations. It seems we're adding another member to our wonderful family."

I release a breath I didn't realize I was holding. My baby is safe. As the weeks pass, the walls around Taurus Terra are constructed, a shield of protection for us all. A steady stream of new minotaurs arrives, enlisted by the Taurus Sentinels to bolster our defenses and safeguard our community.

My belly grows, yet I manage to keep up with the ranch's demands. Each day, I assist Vozak with the various tasks required to tend to our livestock and cultivate our garden. As the season transitions into fall, Auryn patiently teaches me the art of canning the bountiful vegetables and fruits we harvest. We lovingly prepare a care package to send back to our parents, who now reside in the countryside.

Our life here is thriving, a testament to our resilience and unity. As the days unfold, I hold onto the promise of a brighter future for our growing family.

Though my belly grows, my desire to be with Vozak increases. My sex drive is insatiable. He comes to bed after a shower, his body naked and my loins thump with desire. Sitting on the edge of the bed, I smile seductively as he approaches.

"My mate, are you sure all of this mating is safe for the baby?"

"Sara and Jonas assure me it's safe as long as I'm not having complications. Probably best if you stand though."

"Lean back, my love, I'm hungry." He kneels before me, smacking his lips.

My pelvis sizzles as he kisses my lower lips. Pregnancy brings about an increased blood flow there and my senses are heightened. I relish in the surge of utter ecstasy that floods into me. My hands hold onto his horns, holding him to me, while I grind into his face. He moans, loving my reactions. Soon, my pelvis explodes and I arch my back while yelping out through the waves of pleasure which nearly takes my breath away.

I finish and shove him back, his tongue continuing to flick through my soft warm folds. "Again." He lifts long enough to speak and goes back to it. He's stronger than me, and I can't fight it. The over-sensitized sensations are replaced by a strong urge to come again, quicker this time.

"Ahhhhh!" I come again, this time stronger as I buck up and down. As I finish, I back away because after two strong orgasms I can't take it again.

Vozak lifts and laughs at his magical way of doing me twice. He growls, his long, thick cock ready for his turn. I scoot back to the edge of the bed to give him access to what he wants.

He moans as his cock slips into me. I'm very wet after two orgasms and yet his cock still stretches me, filling me. My feet wrap around his waist as he takes hold of my hips, lifting me so he can press into with greater energy.

My body shudders as a third orgasm takes hold, just from him pumping into me. I groan and nearly pass out from the powerful surge of waves passing through my pelvis. The next second, Vozak plunges into me fast and hard, filling me as we rock through the waves of pleasure, until we finish.

I'm an utter ragdoll, unable to move or do anything except catch my breath and let the dizziness and hissing in my ears subside. He chuckles as he crawls onto the bed and pulls me to him at the pillows.

"I don't want to hurt you or the baby. I think we should pull back from doing this until after the baby comes." Vozak's concern rattles me.

I chuckle, unable to stifle my laughter. "I'm sorry, but I can't help it. I just... can't control it."

Vozak grins. "I know, and I enjoy it very much. But we need to ensure the baby's well-being. You do get quite passionate."

I snuggle into his side, his embrace providing comfort. "I love you, Vozak. Thank you for making my dreams come true."

He places a tender kiss on the top of my head. "I love you too, my dear human. Sleep well."

Auryn is three months ahead of me in her pregnancy, and today, we're meant to celebrate the completion of the walls around Taurus Terra. However, Auryn's water breaks just as we're about to leave for the festivities. Of course, I can't leave my sister during this time.

She's already on her bed, perspiring and breathing heavily. Her eyes, wide with a mixture of excitement and apprehension, find mine. "This time feels different. The pains started so quickly after my water broke."

Vozak heads to the wall celebration while I remain by Auryn's side. Soon, Sara and Jonas arrive to assist. With Dario playing in the living room where we can keep watch over him, Vrakius and I support Auryn through her labor.

Janos and Vrakius help Auryn onto her knees, taking advantage of gravity's role in the birthing process. I stand beside Sara as she cleans the baby's head during Auryn's efforts. It's difficult not to share in her pain as she grunts and cries out, but I focus on the baby, whose head emerges into the world. The tiny miracle lets out a hearty cry even before the rest of her body is born, before we even know her gender.

Swiftly, the baby slips into Sara's waiting hands. "It's a girl!" she announces with a smile.

CHAPTER 19

Vozak

The tiny baby girl waves her little hands in the air, her curious eyes absorbing the world around her. Unlike her brother, her head is smooth, lacking the budding horns that suggest Dario will have. He'll be a true minotaur, while she seems to embody a more human appearance. "What's her name?" I inquire, marveling at the delicate features of the newborn.

Agnes gently touches the baby's tiny hands, and the little fingers curl around one of her larger ones. "Pandora Louann," Auryn proudly announces, her smile radiating with maternal joy.

"Ah, Louann is Auryn's middle name," I note, sharing a smile with Agnes.

Auryn nods. "That's right. Minotaurs don't typically have middle names, but we wanted to include a piece of my own heritage."

Agnes continues to caress the baby's soft head. "I love it. Welcome, little Dora."

Auryn's gaze shifts between us. "What about your baby names? Have you two settled on any?"

Agnes and I exchange a glance. "We're working on it," I admit. "We have some ideas, but we're still deciding."

Auryn chuckles. "Well, take your time. I had names picked out because I had to, given the circumstances. But it's wonderful to have choices."

As the weeks pass, Agnes and I embrace the final stages of her pregnancy. Everything progresses smoothly, with the baby's growth and vitals all aligning well. The last trimester comes and goes without too much fuss. However, her due date arrives without any sign of the baby's imminent arrival.

Sara, our trusted medical expert, offers a suggestion. "A bit of intimacy might actually help induce labor."

I blush, feeling a bit flustered. "You mean... that's okay?"

Sara laughs gently. "Of course! Physical intimacy won't harm you or the baby, especially at this point. It might even help trigger labor. Give it a try, and let me know if anything happens."

Agnes grins playfully at me. "Well, don't just stand there. We have a prescription to fill."

With a chuckle, I strip off my clothes. "Anything to help speed things along."

As Agnes undresses, she lies back on the bed, a mischievous glint in her eyes. I quickly join her, eager to follow

Sara's advice. The heightened arousal that comes from this newfound freedom only adds to our passion. Agnes responds fervently to my touch, reaching climax with a shudder.

"Alright, your turn," she playfully demands, a gleam in her eyes. "Don't tell me you can't. Doctor's orders, remember?"

I nod, my desire fueled by both love and the doctor's encouragement. With my cock in my hand, I gently glide it through her wet folds, feeling her readiness. The sensation almost makes me lose control, but I manage to maintain my composure. As I slide into her, her gasp of pleasure confirms that she's more than ready for me.

Her hips move in harmony with my thrusts, her body embracing me in the most intimate way possible. The pleasure is intense, the culmination of shared desire and the urgency of the moment. As I feel myself nearing climax, I let go of any restraint and give in to the overwhelming sensations, both of us finding release in each other's arms.

I lunged forward, my body heaving as the orgasm filled her full. She clung to me, her slickness squeezing me as she came again too. We rock through the undulating waves of pleasure, until I'm empty.

"You're not hurt are you?" I pull back and look at her.

She chuckles playfully. "Am I acting like I'm hurt? No, baby, I think that's exactly what the doctor ordered. Oh." Suddenly, her laughter turns to a grimace as she rolls to her side, clutching her belly. "It's cramping, really bad now!"

In response, I quickly reach for my wrist comm and dial Sara's number. Janos answers the call promptly. "Already?

She's checking on another patient and will be heading home in a few minutes."

"We, well, followed her advice," I confess. "And now Agnes is on her side, holding her belly. She's experiencing a pretty intense cramp."

"That sounds promising. Sounds like labor has started. Good job, Papa. We'll be on our way there." Janos laughs as he concludes the call.

As Agnes lies back on the pillows, now dressed in her gown, I hurriedly put on my clothes. The anticipation of what's to come adds to the excitement and nervousness in the air.

Soon enough, Sara and Janos arrive. Agnes is now at four in terms of her progress. "Looks like we're in for a long night. First-time labors can often take a while. I was in labor for forty-two hours before Pike was born," Sara informs us.

Agnes labors throughout the night, with intermittent periods of sleep in between contractions. Auryn and Dario join us in the morning, bearing freshly baked bread and boiled eggs for breakfast. While Agnes can't find her appetite amidst the labor, the rest of us eagerly consume the food.

The day wears on, and Agnes eventually reaches six in her progress. Sara encourages her to get up and walk around, hoping to encourage her water to break. Agnes steps out onto the porch, gazing wistfully at the fallow garden that will soon need attention as winter takes hold. The air is cool, but not too chilly for a jacket.

"Oh! There goes my water." Agnes stands in a puddle on the porch. She looks up at me apologetically.

"Why apologize?" I put my arm around her and lead her back inside.

"Because I made a mess. Alright. Oh! Ow!" She pauses, gripping a dining chair and leaning over as a contraction grips her with intensity.

Vrakius enters, and Auryn hands off little Dora and Dario to him. "I've got her, you take care of them."

"I'll handle them until Dora needs to eat," Vrakius reassures her. "You focus on Agnes. Let's do this, dear, it's time for you to become a momma!"

Agnes continues to labor for a few more hours, her weariness evident in her eyes. Her face mirrors her yearning for rest, and the labor is beginning to take its toll. She appears on the verge of giving up. I grasp her hand tightly and lean in close.

"Keep going, my love. You're almost there. Sara said you're at nine centimeters now."

"I think it's time to encourage her to get up and let gravity do its work for that last centimeter," Sara suggests. I slip Agnes' arm around my neck, and Janos positions himself on her other side. She's like a delicate burden that we must support, her body limp from the exhaustion.

"I'm so tired. I just want to lie down. Please," Agnes pleads, her voice laden with fatigue.

"No, sweetheart. We need to support you to let the baby come," I assure her, bearing the weight of her weariness against me. Her body trembles in response.

.   .   .

"ALRIGHT, Agnes, it's time to push," Sara directs, positioning herself to catch the baby.

CHAPTER 20

*A*gnes

Summoning every ounce of energy I have left, I push with all my might. Janos and Vozak stand by my side, their strong arms supporting me. Sara's encouraging words fill the air beneath me.

"Push, push, push. That's it, Agnes! You're doing fantastic!"

I continue to push, feeling the baby gradually move through and into Sara's waiting hands. A hearty, healthy cry resounds, and tears of joy well up in my eyes.

"Oh, what a beautiful baby girl!"

Vozak and I exchange tearful glances, overwhelmed with emotion. The medical team gently helps me lie back on the pillows, and Sara places my daughter in my arms. Despite being past my due date, she's small, but her cries are strong and robust.

"It seems like we may have miscalculated your due date," Sara remarks.

I gaze down at my precious girl, noticing the small bumps on her head where her horns will eventually grow. As I rub her tiny head, I glance up at Sara, eager to learn more.

"Some of the halflings have horns, even the females, while others don't. The same goes for the males." Sara imparts her knowledge.

With a natural instinct, my daughter latches onto my breast and begins nursing. Sara and Janos conduct a thorough examination of her after she finishes.

"Despite her smaller size—six pounds—she's incredibly healthy," Janos reports.

Auryn and Vrakius enter the room, congratulating us on the new arrival. Little Dario approaches the bed, his eyes wide with curiosity. "Come, Dario, meet your cousin."

His grin spreads wide as he gently touches the baby's head. "Like Dora," he points out, referencing his baby sister.

I can't help but smile. "Exactly, like Dora! Auryn, they're going to be the best of friends as they grow up."

"Indeed. Now, what is her name?" Auryn inquires.

I look at Vozak, and he nods, signaling that he should be the one to reveal it.

"Fern Madlyn," he announces.

"Fern Madlyn, what a beautiful name! I absolutely love it." Auryn bends down to plant a gentle kiss on Fern's forehead.

As visitors depart, Vozak and I find ourselves alone with our newborn daughter. He's incredibly supportive, allowing me to stay in bed for a few days to rest and tend to Fern's needs. He truly is the best partner.

A week passes, and Vozak is outside tending to ranch chores. I securely wrap Fern in a maya wrap and venture outside, determined to get some exercise and tackle some work in the garden. The time for plowing the soil is approaching, and I walk over the area, knocking down the remnants of last season's plants. Spotting me from the live-stock barn, Vozak heads our way.

"Agnes, what are you two doing out here?" he asks with a hint of concern in his voice.

I smile at his protective nature. "It's sunny, and we both need some fresh air. Just because I've had a baby doesn't mean I can't contribute around here. Fern and I can work together. See, she's snug against me."

Approaching us, he smiles down at our peacefully sleeping daughter. His arms wrap around us both. "I love you both."

"And we love you, Papa." I kiss him affectionately before he returns to his livestock duties.

Being a mother, a wife, and a rancher has given me a new perspective on life. I relish every moment, despite the chal-lenges and occasional communication hurdles we face. It's an ongoing journey filled with love and growth.

"I'd love to take Fern to meet my parents and maybe even head up to New Firelin to see Chelsea. Can we do this before spring gets underway?" I brought up the idea to Vozak, hoping for his agreement.

He contemplates for a moment before giving a thoughtful nod. "I suppose we can arrange a week for that. Flying would save us time. Meeting your parents and your sister sounds like a wonderful plan."

"I'd also love to visit Tariat and meet your parents."

He chuckles softly. "I left that place with hopes of not having to return, but for you, I'd consider it. Maybe we could organize a trip with Vrakius and Auryn after the fall harvest."

"That sounds perfect." I lean in and kiss him, feeling grateful for his willingness to accommodate my wishes. The prospect of traveling and reconnecting with family fills me with excitement. I'm proud of my husband and daughter, and I can't wait to share them with my loved ones.

We nestle into bed, Fern resting in her crib just a few steps away. Moonlight bathes the room in a silvery glow, and I gaze into my husband's eyes. "I've been thinking, maybe in a year or two, Fern could use a little brother or sister. After we've had our time traveling, she celebrates her first birthday."

"Don't rush her growing up too quickly. She's her papa's little girl, and those minotaur horns will set her apart. But otherwise, she's every bit you."

Her spirited attitude and inquisitive nature certainly resemble mine. Before we embark on our travels, a large package arrives addressed to me. It's from the Central Library of Texas, a remnant of the past before the minotaurs' arrival. A few remnants from that time are still preserved in our midst.

Inside the box are numerous books from the library, a thoughtful gesture from both Vozak and Vrakius. I excitedly share this literary treasure with Auryn.

"I plan to teach my children to read in our language. These books are a perfect resource for that," I explain as Dario sits at Auryn's feet, engrossed in a picture book.

"That's a great idea. Perhaps we can form a cooperative effort with others to teach our children about both our history and minotaur history."

"Yes, exactly! I'm grateful you're here. I just wish Chelsea could have married a minotaur too."

I nod in agreement. "Yes, but she's found happiness with Jalen and Sealia. Our niece Sealia is missing out on the minotaur connection."

"We should make a plan to travel to see her and our parents together once a year."

"Absolutely, let's do that."

And with the promise of reunions, we face our bright future, raising our family together.

Be sure to check out Eden's next book in the series: Wed to the Dark Elf

EDEN EMBER

Eden Ember found her passion in writing sci-fi romance. She spends her days either pounding on the keyboard or dreaming up the next stories. Her active imagination never lets up and the perfect outlet comes through in her books.

. . .

Join Eden Ember's exclusive reader's list

- New Books, Hot Sales, and Freebies
- Eden's reader giveaways
- EXCLUSIVE sneak peeks at upcoming novels
- First look at Covers
- Who Eden Recommends (Love me some SCI FI Romance!)

EdenEmber.com

Eden Ember on FaceBook

Follow Eden Ember on Amazon

Follow Eden Ember on BookBub

ARRANGED MONSTER MATES

Series Page is HERE

Wed to the Ice Giant by Layla Fae

Wed to the Minotaur by Eden Ember

Wed to the Wolfman by Cara Wylde

Wed to the Phoenix by Eden Ember

Wed to the Dragon by Cara Wylde

Wed to the Orc by Layla Fae

Wed to the Lionman by Cara Wylde

Wed to the Lich by Layla Fae

Wed to the Bullman by Eden Ember

Wed to Jack Frost by Layla Fae

Wed to the Dark Elf by Eden Ember

Wed to Krampus by Cara Wylde

Printed in Dunstable, United Kingdom